THE RELIC OF POWER

THE RELIC OF POWER

KEENON SOLOMON

Published by Mynd Matters Publishing
201 17th Street NW, Suite 300, Atlanta, GA 30363
www.myndmatterspublishing.com

Library of Congress Control Number: 2018957399
ISBN-13: 978-1-948145-12-1

FIRST EDITION

Printed in the United States of America

Dedicated to my loving mother,

Melody Fleming.

Table of Contents

CHAPTER 1

THE AMAZING RONALD MOORE

New York City is home to millions of people and hundreds of places, but one place almost everyone has been is The Museum of Important Artifacts. Although what's inside brings people from far and near, most want to get a glimpse of Ronald Moore, the man who single-handedly secured half of the artifacts on display. When the world-renowned artifact collector isn't on the hunt for his next extraordinary find, Ronald usually spends his time giving tours of the museum. The reaction people have as they fall all over themselves to ask him questions gives him a sense of accomplishment and inflates his already substantial ego.

As Ronald excitedly told a group of museum tourists about some of his most recent findings, his co-worker, Robert, interrupted him.

"The boss wants to meet with you," Robert said urgently.

Instantly, Ronald's joyful expression disappeared. He believed his time at the museum was constantly tied up with tedious tasks that never allowed him to do simple things, like sharing his experiences with a group of intrigued tourists. Sometimes he secretly wished he could lighten his workload, but he'd never admit it. Ronald thought being the best meant taking on every challenge the only way he knew how—alone with no help. Yet, there were times he'd have to bite the bullet and pick his battles wisely. Robert's raised brow and solemn expression told him this was one of those times.

"It's serious," Robert assured him as if he could sense Ronald's agitation. "Head to his office. I'll finish the tour."

Ronald placed his hand on Robert's shoulder and nodded thankfully before making his way to his boss' office.

He arrived at the dull grey room, decorated with scholastic plaques, certificates, and framed article clippings. The man responsible for the showcased successes was stationed behind a large mahogany desk, firmly planted in the middle of the room. Ronald took a seat, prepared for his typical interactions with the boss.

"What do you need, Martin?" Ronald asked, paring his question with an annoyed sigh.

Martin Roche, the museum curator, and Ronald had a long-standing, if not sometimes strained, relationship.

"You can start with showing me some respect," Martin answered. "After all, you work for me."

"You know I mean no harm," Ronald wore a playful grin to lighten the mood before cutting to the chase. "So, what do you need me to do?"

"We've been called into an urgent mission and

it has your name written all over it," Martin responded.

As always, Ronald's first question was "Where?" But this time, Martin's response wasn't a location. Instead, he hit Ronald with an unexpected request.

"You're not going to like it Ronald but I need you to have a partner on this one."

Ronald was immediately caught off guard and filled with confusion.

"Martin, you've assigned me countless missions where I never needed a partner and we have a museum full of artifacts to prove it. What makes this one so different?"

Martin leaned forward in his seat and sighed as he stared at Ronald with a look of seriousness.

"This might be the most dangerous mission out there."

"I've been on plenty of "dangerous" missions alone and have the scars to prove it. You still haven't told me what makes this one any different," Ronald declared, frustration building in his voice.

"Ronald, I need you to cooperate," Martin's attempt to stabilize the situation only irritated Ronald more.

"Why? I'm the greatest explorer you have! I know how to do my job better than any explorer you've ever come across and yet, you still haven't told me one reason why I can't handle this mission alone," Ronald snapped as he rose from his seat. "What's the mission?"

"SIT DOWN!" Martin's booming voice bounced off the office walls as the two men stared at one another, tension building around them.

Martin pressed his fingertips against his temples and emitted a deep sigh before breaking the silence.

"Listen, I am not questioning your ability. If I didn't think you could handle the challenge, I wouldn't have called you in here in the first place. Another set of eyes will be helpful this time around and I'm not willing to compromise. Are you in or not?"

Ronald slowly retook his seat while listening to Martin's words and processing the means of his request. He knew he had to swallow his pride to make it work. He still couldn't understand the need for a partner, but he had no reason to go against Martin's wishes. He had to trust his boss even if he felt the request was ridiculous and unnecessary.

"You sure do get cranky for an old man," Ronald surrendered through a light joke, timidly placing his hand on the back of his head. "So, when do I meet this *partner*?"

A satisfied grin formed on Martin's face.

"I thought you'd never ask. Follow me."

With Ronald finally on board, the two walked to the other side of the museum until they reached the Worldview Exhibit. The average visitor was always amazed to find some of the most breathtaking historical artifacts in the world within its walls. Yet, behind a door cautioning museum goers that they were entering a restricted area, and down a narrow hallway, was a special room with a lifetime of secrets. Martin's "mission room" was filled with finds too sacred to display. The walls were covered with surveillance maps and monitors and a long table extending across a back wall held multiple computers with tracking devices and biometric scanners. It was also where Ronald and Martin discussed the details of top secret missions.

Instantly, Ronald spotted a tall, brunette woman admiring one of the monitors. He rolled his eyes before elbowing Martin in the arm.

"That's what you call a partner? A star struck tourist? Is her height supposed to protect us?" Ronald muttered low enough for only Martin to hear.

Martin exhaled deeply. He had already prepared for Ronald's constant barrage of slick comments and could only hope that the lack of hospitality wouldn't push his new explorer away.

"Ms. Klein," Martin called, gaining the

woman's attention. She turned to reveal a warm smile filled with curiosity.

"Please call me Susan," she insisted, exposing her British accent. She held out her hand while walking towards Ronald.

"You must be Ronald," she said as she greeted him.

Ronald hesitated only slightly before shaking her hand.

"It's nice to meet you, Mr. Moore. I've heard wonderful things about you."

"Thank you," Ronald responded dryly. "I'm sure you could give history lessons on the artifacts I've brought into this museum. What are you, a schoolteacher?"

Susan was immediately taken aback by his arrogance and rude demeanor. She prepared herself to meet a man that many would describe as an inspirational hero, not a jerk. Determined to keep her composure and professionalism, she continued to smile as she gave her response.

"Why, you are absolutely correct, Mr. Moore. My students would say I give fantastic history lessons, those of which have prepared me to go on this mission with you. You do want a knowledgeable partner, don't you?"

Ronald could already tell the two were bound to bump heads. The mere excitement in her voice agitated him, let alone her snippy retort.

"To be honest with you *Susan,* I would prefer not having a partner at all, but here you are," he shot back.

"Alright, that's quite enough," Martin intervened while cutting a stern look at Ronald.

"We are both very intrigued by the new perspective you're bringing to the team, Susan," Martin assured her.

"Now that we've gotten introductions out of the way, let's get down to business."

Ronald and Susan took their seats at the round oak conference table while Martin stood, facing a high-tech monitor displaying an interactive map.

"For this mission, you guys have to find a very powerful and rare relic, *The Relic of Power*. You'll board a plane to Yakutsk, Siberia. Approximately one mile from where you're dropped off, you will meet Melody at the rendezvous spot, a café in a nearby town. She will tell you the relic's location, what it can do, and how to get it."

"When do we take off?" Susan interjected enthusiastically.

"The plane should be here in roughly two hours," Martin answered before giving Ronald a digital map of Yakutsk. "You're in charge of this mission but that doesn't mean she's not your partner."

"You can trust me Martin. *The Relic of Power* will be here in no time," Ronald assured him.

Martin gave Ronald a nod of approval before giving them further instructions. "Go home, pack your things, and be back here in two hours. The plane will be waiting out back. It's go time."

As Ronald rose from his seat, Susan reached

out and touched his shoulder, stopping him in his tracks.

"I can't wait to get started!"

Instead of returning her enthusiasm, Ronald glanced at her with an awkward smile.

"This is going to be a long mission," he mumbled as they exited the room.

CHAPTER 2

OPPOSITES

Exactly two hours later, Ronald and Susan met Martin near the small runway behind the museum. Martin didn't exchange many words with Ronald as the well-seasoned explorer entered the team's private jet. As Susan prepared to walk up the stairs and join Ronald on the plane, Martin tapped her on the shoulder. She looked back, still sporting an optimistic smile.

"This mission will not be easy—on many levels. Remember your objective and why you chose to be an explorer. Don't let what happens out there change you. Also, be careful and I wish you the best of luck," Martin's intention was to make sure Ronald's ego hadn't already discouraged her.

"Thank you," Susan responded before running

up the steps.

Externally, Susan hadn't shown an ounce of doubt. But inside, her gut was overflowing with fear. She knew all the research in the world couldn't compare to experience. With each step, she questioned her decision to commit to the mission. Yet, she maintained a resilient attitude, despite Ronald's discouraging first impression.

Aboard the plane, Ronald wasted no time taking his seat. He was used to Martin's sophisticated taste in aircrafts but noticed that Susan seemed to be in awe as her eyes roamed every inch of the capacious jet. *If she opens her mouth any wider, her jaw is going to hit the floor,* thought Ronald.

"You've never been on a private plane before?" he asked incredulously.

"I've never been on one this big!" Susan replied, bewilderment gleaming in her eyes.

It dawned on Ronald that everything astounded her and they hadn't even made it to their destination.

"Susan, have you ever retrieved an artifact?" he questioned, narrowing his eyes.

Susan knew the question would come eventually. Yet, her heart still managed to sink into the pit of her stomach. It was obvious Ronald had a huge ego and wasn't excited about her tagging along. She was certain if he found out she's an amateur, he would freak. Regardless, she couldn't lie to him.

"No, this is my first mission," she responded dryly. As expected, Ronald was outraged.

"I can't believe Martin would partner me with an amateur! I thought I was going to find an artifact. Babysitting was not part of the plan."

Hearing his harsh words struck a sour note with Susan. Obviously, being nice wouldn't cut it.

"You're not babysitting anyone!" Susan snapped. "We are both adults and should treat each other like equal partners."

Ronald suddenly became even more annoyed

with the idea of being *equal* with someone else on a mission, especially a schoolteacher with no prior experience.

"I've been doing this for eleven years and this is your first time. Clearly, we are not equal. I'm in charge here and what I say goes."

Susan chuckled at Ronald's demand before stepping closer to him, so the two were eye to eye.

"I'm no one's sidekick and you're not going to boss me around. You will listen to what I have to say, just as I will do for you. Understand?"

Ronald smirked at his ability to crack her positive façade. Her attempt to be assertive was interesting but he still felt there was no room for two leaders on the mission.

After a brief pause, Ronald replied with a dismissive shake of his head.

"No," he slipped a pair of headphones over his ears and closed his eyes.

Irate and distraught at his childish behavior, Susan took her seat across from his and tried to calm herself. After a long period of silence, she felt the need to say something.

"Are you going to ignore me for the rest of the mission?"

"If I can," Ronald responded, nonchalantly.

Susan was outraged.

"Just because this is my first mission doesn't mean you have the right to mistreat me!"

Ronald decided the conversation was over. He hoped ignoring her would make it clear.

"Stubborn jerk," Susan mumbled.

"Whiny brat," Ronald retorted.

"I don't have to take any of this from you!"

"Well then leave!" Ronald shouted, hoping there was a way she could catch the next jet back to New York.

"The only way for me to leave is to jump off of this plane, so you're stuck with me."

"I'm not stuck with anyone," said Ronald.

With an even stronger desire to end the pointless argument once and for all, he rose from his seat and walked to the rear of the plane where he figured he could rest without having to bicker for the remainder of the flight.

Ronald woke and looked out of the window to see an icy, isolated landscape. He immediately knew it was Siberia because he'd been there before. Nothing about it had been pleasant considering he was in an icy forest, constantly aware of the threat of wolves and tigers.

After taking the last shower he'd have for days, Ronald felt prepared for the first day of the mission. That was, until Susan confronted him.

"What happened yesterday should really—"

"I don't want to hear it," he interrupted before walking off.

Susan began to lose her spirit and the real mission hadn't even begun.

CHAPTER 3

THE MISSION

A few hours had passed since Ronald and Susan's last encounter. They hadn't seen or talked to one another since. As the plane began its descent, the reality of having to drag around what he considered to be a useless addition settled in for Ronald. He was determined not to allow his new circumstances to put a dent in his reputation. After all, the amazing Ronald Moore could do anything, and this wasn't an exception.

Similarly, Susan knew working with Ronald would be challenging, but it had to be done. That reality was the only thing the two had in common. While they realized they weren't happy to be stuck together, the mission wasn't about their feelings. It was about retrieving *The Relic of Power*.

When they finally landed on the icy tundra of

Siberia, Ronald and Susan grabbed their bags and deplaned. Susan thanked the pilot while Ronald walked right passed him.

Once they entered the town, they noticed very few people roaming around the streets.

"The café where we meet Melody is two blocks from here," Ronald informed Susan as he checked the map Martin had given him.

They walked in silence until they reached the café. When they walked inside, Susan scanned the patrons, struggling to pick Melody out from the crowd. However, Ronald detected the nondescript woman as if she stuck out like a sore thumb. Melody sat at a small round table along the back wall wearing a navy blue hooded sweatshirt and drinking a cup of tea. Ronald headed towards her as Susan followed closely behind.

"I was worried your partner was going to yell my name in order to find me," Melody joked.

Ronald grinned at the spy's observation. "Well, she's a bit of an amateur so it's to be expected.

Either way, I'll do all the talking."

His comment angered Susan but she remained composed.

Melody looked over at Susan somewhat sympathetically before returning her eyes to Ronald.

"Okay then," Melody said as she sipped her tea and began explaining the details of their new mission.

"*The Relic of Power* is an archaic relic dating back thousands of generations. In the wrong hands, it destroyed entire civilizations and left families in ruin. *The Relic of Power* can also create endless peace and stability but it keeps ending up in the hands of dictators that rarely want peace and instead choose to harness the relic's power only for personal gain. Our job is to retrieve it from the Kingdom of Zandina and take it to the museum where it can be kept under safe lock and key and cause no more harm."

"Where exactly is Zandina?" asked Ronald.

"Over the Belukha Mountains. We'll have a plane take you there but once you land, you're on your own. The ancient civilization lies just beyond the mountains. *The Relic of Power* will probably be with the highest authority, so your goal is to find him. You'll know what to do when you do. Remember, if anything happens, including your death, all records that you were on this mission will be erased."

Melody sipped more tea before asking, "All clear?"

"Well, no," said Susan, "Are we going to go there and steal it from them?"

"In short, yes. The leader of Zandina wants to expand his territory and extract all of its power so he can use it for his own benefit. The expansion and his wicked plans would destroy communities, kill families and animals, and give him unlimited power and control. If we take it, the relic won't do any harm. Because once *The Relic of Power* is away from its homeland, its powerless."

As Susan prepared to ask another question, Ronald shot her a look and instead, she refrained.

"Let's go. I'll give you a ride to the chopper," Melody said as she finished her tea, stood, and placed a few coins on the table.

In the car, Ronald sat in the front seat, while Susan sat in the back.

"So how long have you been working with the museum?" Susan asked Melody.

"Seventeen years," Melody responded. Susan hoped the conversation would continue, but it didn't so she went back to looking out the window.

"We have to drop you at the top of the mountain, so there's climbing gear inside," Melody informed them once they reached the helicopter.

"Thank you," Susan said as she entered the helicopter.

Though the ride wouldn't be long, Ronald and Susan drifted to sleep as they headed to the Belukha Mountains.

CHAPTER 4

THE LAND OF ZANDINA

Ronald woke as they approached the Belukha Mountains, precisely two hours after takeoff.

"We're almost there, Mr. Moore. You should wake your partner," the pilot suggested.

Ronald hesitated to say anything to Susan. While there was no doubt in his mind that she would only cause trouble, he couldn't leave her on the helicopter.

"Wake up. We're here," Ronald said dryly as he tapped her shoulder.

Susan stirred once she felt Ronald's taps.

As soon as the helicopter landed on top of the mountains, they unbuckled their straps and grabbed their climbing gear.

"Good luck out there," said the pilot.

"Thanks but we don't need luck. At least I don't," Ronald retorted, cutting his eyes at Susan.

"Great way to encourage your partner," Susan muttered sarcastically.

Ronald ignored her comment and stepped down with Susan not far behind.

A lump of fear grew in Susan's throat as she looked at the mountain.

"We have to go down that?" she asked pointing.

"Yep," Ronald responded nonchalantly. "It shouldn't be that hard for you. You're my knowledgeable and well-prepared partner, remember."

"Of course not. I'll be fine," Susan said, trying to sound as confident as possible even though she was petrified.

Ronald rappelled down the mountain and was able to move swiftly around the rocky terrain while

Susan lagged behind.

"I'm a 40-year-old man," Ronald shouted so Susan could hear him. "You shouldn't have any problems keeping up."

"This is my first time going down a mountain," Susan shouted back.

"I really don't understand why he chose you," Ronald mumbled.

Though his words cut like a knife, Susan knew the only way to shut him up was to prove him wrong. She did her best to keep up with him. Although she couldn't catch him, she kept gaining ground and inched closer and closer.

For several yards, she remained close, but an attempt to go over a curvy rock caused her to fall.

Ronald jumped on a large rock, took out his rope, and yelled to Susan, "Catch it!"

She extended her hand, barely grabbing the rope. She gripped it with her other hand and Ronald pulled her up slowly.

When Susan got close enough to him, he told

her to take his hand. Their fingertips met and Ronald pulled her up and onto the rock beside him.

"Don't try to catch up with me. Stay at your own pace even if it's slow," Ronald scolded.

His advice landed on deaf ears. She knew keeping up was the only way to earn his respect.

After nearly an hour of going down the mountain, a mist filled the air. They were officially in the land of Zandina.

"What is this?" Ronald said as he walked into a humid jungle full of multi-colored plants and trees, different types of birds and wildlife, and plenty of bugs. Confused, he stopped in his tracks. They had just come from the icy terrain of the Belukha Mountains, the exact opposite of this new terrain. *Is this the work of The Relic of Power?*

After a few minutes, Susan finally met him at the bottom of the mountain.

"Is this Zandina?" She asked matching

Ronald's earlier disbelief. This time he understood why she was baffled yet amazed.

"I think so," he replied.

"It's beautiful," Susan said as she plucked a nearby flower.

"We should get to work. Let's go." Ronald explored the jungle as Susan trailed closely behind.

As they walked, Susan had to constantly flick bugs from her arms and legs. Although she figured it would be uncomfortable at times, she grew annoyed with how many bugs there were and how ill-prepared she felt.

"Will these bugs just go away?" she asked aloud to no one in particular.

"Stop complaining," Ronald muttered, rolling his eyes.

As they stepped deeper into the jungle, Susan asked, "Have you ever gone through a jungle before?"

"I'm an explorer. Of course I have."

They continued, the whole time being swarmed

by bugs and dodging dangerous wildlife. Everything seemed to be going well until Ronald heard a noise.

"Wait! Stay still," Ronald said to Susan as they ducked behind a tree. They stood completely still for a couple of minutes until a wolf-like dog came into view, barking and likely alerting whoever was following its lead.

"Run!" Ronald instructed Susan.

The creature chased them, soon joined by two more beasts. Ronald climbed up a neighboring tree and as Susan tried to join, one of the animals latched onto her leg, it's sharp canines sinking into her calf, refusing to let go.

"Ronald help!" She screamed as she tried to fight off the hound.

Ronald pulled his gun from the holster and shot the creature squarely between the eyes. With little time to spare, Susan pushed the dead carcass off of her leg before running from the other two mutated hybrids.

Ronald shot at the beasts, hitting one in the leg. Before he could shoot the other, the tree branch he'd been sitting on broke. He braced himself for the fall before landing on his back. He covered his face as the third dog growled and clawed at him.

Ronald groaned in pain as the wolf-like hound scratched and clawed at his skin. He grabbed its paw and threw the animal to the ground. While trying to stand up, the dog tackled him.

"Help!" He shouted as he tried to keep the beast from biting and scratching him more. Susan ran over and immediately shot the dog before helping Ronald get to his feet.

"Good job," Ronald said while trying to catch his breath.

"Thanks," Susan responded. "Are you sure we should stay here? Someone must have heard those gunshots."

"We have no choice. We have to find the relic and we're not leaving until we do."

They continued trekking through the jungle

until they heard nearby leaves rustling.

"Get out your gun and stay low," Ronald whispered.

The rustling continued as men in red and white battle armor exited the bushes. They carried spears, swords, staffs, and daggers, all aimed at Ronald and Susan. As they formed a circle and closed in around them, Ronald shot one of the soldiers in the chest. One soldier charged at Ronald with his dagger but Ronald bent down, firing two shots in rapid succession, hitting him in the stomach. While he was focused on that soldier, two others came behind him, ready to attack. Fortunately, Susan covered him and shot them both, stopping them in their tracks.

"Look out!" Ronald yelled as a soldier came behind her with a sword.

The soldier swung his sword at her head, but she ducked and shot him. Another soldier charged at her with a spear. She fired her weapon but nothing happened. She looked down and realized she was out of ammo. She took off running as fast as she could, away from the soldiers. As she ran, another soldier with a staff hit her in the head, knocking her unconscious.

As the soldier with the spear grabbed Susan, Ronald shot him. Then, the soldier with the staff charged at him so Ronald pointed his gun and pulled the trigger. *Click, click.* He looked down to confirm that he was also out of ammo. He threw his gun at the soldier, slowing him down. Ronald and the soldier charged one another. As Ronald came within a few feet of the soldier, he was hit with a staff and knocked unconscious.

CHAPTER 5

MEETING THE KING

Ronald woke up to find himself strapped to a chair. Groggy, he stretched his neck from side to side as his eyes adjusted to the light. The expansive room contained ten white ionic columns, five on each side. Massive flags with stripes of red, white, and orange hung across each set. The ceilings were painted in similar colors with gold outlines and etchings. His head fell and his eyes landed on the plush red carpet that ran from one entry point to a massive chair atop three steps. He searched his memory trying to place the décor in a recent photo he'd seen but couldn't remember.

He heard a grunt and glanced across the room to see Susan also strapped to a chair.

"Are you okay?" she asked worriedly.

"I'm fi-," Ronald started before being

interrupted.

"Silence!" A man in stately attire bellowed as he entered the room followed by four guards.

"The throne room!" Ronald said, pleased with himself for remembering the image Melody had shown them.

The King of Zandina stared at them intensely as he inspected them closely.

"Why are you here?" he asked.

"We're here to-" Susan stopped abruptly as she made eye contact with Ronald.

The King approached her and grabbed her by the neck.

"I will ask again. Why are you here?" Susan remained quiet. The King tightened his grip around her neck waiting for her to beg for his mercy.

"She doesn't know anything," Ronald said capturing the King's attention.

"This is the last time I will ask. Why. Are. You. Here?" The King placed both hands around

Ronald's neck and squeezed even tighter. Sensing that Ronald had something to say, the King removed his hands and waited for a response.

"To see how many chins you have," Ronald retorted, flashing a grin through coughs as he tried to catch his breath. Susan suppressed laughter as the King grew noticeably angry.

"You come here and disrespect me?" He took out his knife and slashed Ronald's face. "Where did you come from, you scum?" Ronald didn't answer. The King raised his knife, nearly stabbing Ronald in the eye.

"America," Ronald admitted.

"Of course you filthy Americans would come here and disrespect my honor."

Ronald parted his lips to speak, but this time Susan flashed him a look that made him hold his tongue.

"Zandina was once a dominant kingdom admired by all for its vast beauty and resources. We were a superpower until someone stole what was rightfully ours and left us to waste, ruining everything our forefathers fought for. We had nothing left but knew if we got back our power, we would one day rule the world. *The Relic of Power* is where it belongs and I vow that it will forever remain on this hallowed ground. We will expand our territory and not even you, *Americans*, will destroy our plan."

Ronald and Susan looked at one another with raised eyebrows and then back to the King.

"I know why you two are here. You want my power. You want what is Zandina's. But you will not have it because it does not belong to you," said the King as he paced back and forth between the two. "*The Relic of Power* feeds off of the desires of the land. Since I rule the land, it is mine and only mine to control." The King spoke with a blend of authority and disgust.

"But we didn't ruin this land, you did. You stole from your own people and tried to control them with the relic's power. You are the enemy of

Zandina, not us," said Susan boldly.

The King walked towards her with rage in his eyes.

"You accuse me of stealing? You know nothing! I took what was owed to me and my family."

"Through murder!" argued Susan. "You killed hundreds of people on this hallowed land, as you called it, just so you could be the King. You aren't the rightful King of Zandina.

Ronald stared at Susan surprised by her knowledge and forcefulness. While he gained some respect for her, the King became more incensed by her accusations and blatant disrespect.

"Enough with you! I will show you who is the rightful King of Zandina. You both will die by public execution tomorrow. Until then, take them to the dungeon!"

CHAPTER 6

PRISON BREAK

The King's guards threw Ronald and Susan into an isolated underground prison cell just beneath the King's castle. Two guards were left to stand watch.

"I knew I shouldn't have become an explorer," Susan said, panicking. "I'm going to die on my first mission."

"Don't worry, I'll find a way to get us out of here."

Instead of providing solace, Ronald's words angered Susan.

"You're not a superhero!" Susan yelled. "You can't fly us out of here. Let's face it, we're gonna die."

Ronald was taken aback by her tone because for once, he meant well by his statement. He felt it was his duty to make sure they both got out of there alive. He shrugged off her doubts and tried his best not to become bitter.

"Susan, the chances of us getting out of this prison are pretty slim but we'll find a way. Just trust me, okay."

They sat in silence, allowing a blend of tension and tiredness to overcome them.

"Do you trust me with your life?" Ronald asked. Susan searched her thoughts for an appropriate and honest response.

Finally, she answered, "I don't know. Should I?"

For the first time in his life, Ronald was at a loss for words.

"Let's find a way to get out of here," he said.

Susan remained planted, displeased with Ronald's decision to ignore her question. "Can I trust you with my life Ronald? After all, you're the one who brought it up."

"I honestly don't know," he said. "I try not to

worry about anyone but myself. It's been easier to live that way."

"But things are different now. We're partners so my fate is your fate and vice versa," Susan responded.

Ronald paused, his eyes cemented on the prison floor. "Let's just get out of here, okay?"

Susan nodded, realizing that Ronald was probably never going to change.

"First, we'll need a distraction and some kind of weapon," Ronald said.

"I have an idea," Susan stated but Ronald quickly dismissed her help.

"Just let me think of it," said Ronald distracted.

"That's your problem!" Susan yelled. "You think you're perfect at everything when you're not. If there is one thing I hate, it's working with a know-it-all!"

Ronald frowned and replied, "Maybe I wouldn't be such a know-it-all if I had a partner that could actually *do* something."

In a fit of rage, Susan slapped Ronald, catching them both by surprise. Shocked, neither moved nor said a word for several seconds.

"I'm so sorry," Susan apologized profusely. She'd crossed a line by hitting Ronald regardless of his insults or her anger.

Ronald shoved her backwards into the nearest wall. "Don't ever touch me again."

Forgetting the remorse she'd felt only moments before, she growled, "I hate you."

They moved to separate ends of the cell and sat with their backs facing the other until they both fell asleep.

From the padded window, Ronald saw signs of early morning and assumed they were two hours from execution. Instead of waking Susan, he walked around the cell looking for something, anything, to use as a weapon. After searching for a few minutes, he found what appeared to be a bone, probably from some long forgotten previous occupant of the same cell. Momentarily shaken at the thought, Ronald proceeded to sharpen it against a concrete wall, fashioning a sharp edge.

He did his best to shave the bone without taking up too much time. An hour later, Ronald figured his new weapon could be used with the right amount of pressure despite its small, dull point.

"Susan, wake up," Ronald nudged her. "What time is it?" she asked.

"I'll tell you later," he said. "Until then, I need you to fake your death."

"Why?" she asked. Irritated, Ronald rolled his eyes. "Will you just do it? I'll call the guard over here and stab him with this," he showed Susan the sharpened bone.

"Okay," Susan agreed without question.

Susan fell back as Ronald shouted, "Help! Someone help! She's dying!"

"Hush your mouth, boy!" One of the guards

yelled.

Ronald wanted to hit him for calling him a boy, but instead he asked, "Can you help? My friend is dying."

Seeing Susan on the floor, the guard opened the cell door and quickly rushed over to her to inspect her closely. Within seconds, Ronald stabbed him twice in the side. As the guard doubled over in pain while screaming in agony, Ronald clutched the makeshift weapon tightly between his fingers awaiting the footsteps of the other guard. The second guard rushed into the cell and immediately ran towards the first guard asking what happened. Ronald grabbed the guard's spear from behind and struck him on the head knocking him unconscious.

"Where's our stuff?" Ronald asked reverting his attention back to the first guard who was struggling trying to nurse his gushing wound. The guard lay slumped, staring at Ronald in silent defiance.

Ronald returned his steely glance. "If you want a chance at survival...," he threatened.

There was no need to finish the threat.

"In the King's treasury. Down the hall and to the left from the throne room."

Ronald tossed the guard an old, discarded rag.

"Apply pressure," stated Ronald as he pulled Susan up on her feet and they ran out of the cell.

CHAPTER 7
INFILTRATION

"How are we going to get to the treasury without getting caught?" Susan asked.

"That's a good question," Ronald replied as they both pondered solutions.

"Wait a minute, I've got it! We can pretend to be the guards."

"How are you going to fit into their uniform?" Ronald inquired.

"I won't," she said as she headed back towards the cell. "I'll be the prisoner, while you will be the guard."

This was the moment Ronald never saw coming. A proverbial blindfold was ripped off of his eyes. While it had never been a problem for him to dismiss the idea of a partner before, he had also never been in a position that made his brain power seem so miniscule. Without Susan's help, getting out of sticky situations would be harder and he could no longer convince himself otherwise. It was a relieving feeling that somehow left a nasty taste in Ronald's mouth. Anyone else might have taken this realization in stride, but Ronald's resilient ego wasn't fading without a fight.

"That's not half bad rookie, but don't expect to have any more rock star ideas."

Both guards were still on the ground, one unconscious and the other passed out from the loss of blood. Ronald removed the headgear from the first guard along with his uniform.

"Desperate times call for desperate measures after all."

Susan paused, taking a deep breath to stop herself from exploding. *Even when he's admitting I'm right, he's a jerk!* She thought to herself. It took her a few seconds to shove her bubbling emotions and growing regret to the back of her mind. By the time she managed to collect herself, Ronald had already changed into the first guard's uniform.

"How do I look?" Ronald asked.

"Like a pillock," Susan responded before walking off to put on a pair of handcuffs that had been hanging beside the cell door. Ronald didn't know Susan had just called him an idiot, but he was for certain that her British slang was not nice.

Once they were both suited up, they headed out of the prison and back towards the castle. Ronald glanced over at Susan.

"You're not worried?"

"No, I'm not," intense sarcasm and sass oozed from her response.

"That's interesting. Normally you would be worrying or whining in this sort of situation," Ronald shot back with ease, knowing he could surpass her sarcasm without trying.

"Well I…" Before Susan could spit out another comment, Ronald lifted a finger causing her to pause. They were standing in front of the King's castle and it was time to get serious.

"Okay, I need you to look angry and don't say a word," Susan nodded at Ronald's instructions as they headed into the castle.

As they approached the entryway, one of the guards narrowed his eyes at Ronald and placed his hand on his shoulder.

"What happened to your suit?"

Confused, Ronald looked down at the uniform he'd quickly thrown on and noticed two large holes surrounded by blood.

"This scum tried to escape!" Ronald said as he pulled Susan's hair. She winced in pain as he yanked her past the guard and pushed her down a long hallway. They encountered several more guards who appeared less interested in Ronald's uniform or his prisoner. Retracing their steps from the day before, they continued through one opulent room after another before finally entering the throne room.

In the center of the room, the portly King sat on his throne, a grim look of disappointment and disgust visible on his face. He slowly stood and approached Ronald.

"Do you have no respect?"

"Yes, my King. I have only respect for you my King," Ronald replied in a British accent.

"Kneel!" yelled the King as he became increasingly frustrated by his guard's unusual behavior.

Ronald did as he was told and kept his head bowed towards the King's feet.

"Why did you bring her here?"

"This filthy American tried to escape. She stabbed me in the chest," Ronald responded.

"What happened to the other American?"

"I had to kill him after he attacked and killed one of us."

The King turned his attention to Susan.

"You dishonored me yesterday with your lies. Now, it's time for you to get the same treatment as your friend," The King pulled a knife from his jacket and ran the blade along Susan's jawline. He moved in closer and whispered, "You were right. I did what I had to do to become King. But regardless of what I did, I am the ruler of Zandina and the rightful owner of *The Relic of Power*. You failed and now you must die."

As the King focused on Susan, Ronald repositioned a spear in his right hand and as the King turned around, he pierced him in his side. The King stumbled towards his throne, feeling at the deep cut in his side. Ronald sliced off Susan's handcuffs just as the King's guards raised their spears and pointed them at the pair. The King fell only steps before he reached his throne, bleeding and mumbling. Several guards entered the room and ran to his side. As he convulsed on the ground, the guards were angered and attacked Susan and Ronald.

Susan grabbed the King's knife from where it had fallen and fended off two of the guards by stabbing one in the chest and dodging an attack from the other. The remaining guard pierced

Susan's arm as she wounded him in the leg. Another guard tried to attack Susan from behind but Ronald circled around and caught him with the spear. Susan slammed one guard to the ground and Ronald punched him in the chest.

"Watch out!" Susan yelled as a spear flew towards Ronald. He caught it and hurled it back at the guard, hitting him in the shoulder.

Castle guards and Zandinan soldiers came from every entry point. Ronald and Susan ran from one hallway to another, looking for the treasury but finding only more attacks. They fought and fought until they finally reached what had to be the treasury.

As they stepped inside, a guard tackled Susan and two soldiers attacked Ronald. He kicked one guard in the gut and stuck the other with his spear. Suddenly, Susan fell to the ground. Ronald looked over to see the stab wound in her arm. Ronald threw a spear at the guard standing over Susan's wounded body. Feeling defenseless and unprotected, Ronald looked around for another weapon but saw nothing in sight. He raised his fists prepared to fight.   One soldier tripped him and pinned him to the floor while the other smiled as he lowered the spear, ready to push it deep into Ronald's side. Out of nowhere, the smiling guard groaned and fell to the ground. The other tried to shift his position as Susan stood over him, spear in hand. Before he could reach for a weapon, Ronald head-butted him and pushed him backwards onto Susan's waiting spear.

"You owe me one," she said as she pulled him up and they ran to find the treasury.

The treasury contained a multitude of artifacts and riches. They saw endless jewels, weapons, ancient paintings, and their equipment. Just as Susan was about to ask Ronald how to find *The Relic of Power*, she looked up and saw a prism-shaped glass case, outlined in gold trim, with a sphere the size of her fist nestled inside. *The Relic of*

Power was held in place by a six-legged brass stand attached to the base of the case. Engravings of tribal symbols covered *The Relic of Power's* exterior and surrounded the oval amber gem plunged in the center. It possessed a pulsing yellow and orange glow, adding to its breathtaking beauty.

"How amazing is this!" Susan exclaimed. "It's right here. I can't believe they don't have it locked up or something." She lifted the top of the case and removed it with every ounce of carefulness she could muster. Upon connecting with Susan's hand, *The Relic of Power's* inner light dimmed. Just as Susan began to ask Ronald about it, she heard an alarm sound off in the distance. Susan carefully placed *The Relic of Power* into her backpack.

"I doubt they believed someone would try to take it. Regardless, get your head out of the clouds," Ronald said sharply. "Those soldiers will be here any minute."

Ronald removed the guard's armor and threw on the extra shirt and pants he'd packed. He reloaded his gun and tucked it inside his backpack along with the map.

"I'm ready," Susan said after getting dressed and moving towards the exit. Ronald joined her and they cautiously peeked down the hallway to spot any of the King's men that may have been waiting nearby.

"How are we going to get out of here?" whispered Susan.

Ronald's eyes darted back and forth across the room searching for an escape.

"We're going to break that window by jumping through it," said Ronald casually.

"We don't have to break it," said Susan confused. "We can just open it."

"But that takes the fun out of it," Ronald said as he pulled up the latch and opened the window.

Susan climbed out and Ronald followed closely behind. He closed the window just as Susan remembered the mission.

"We forgot *The Relic of Power*!"

"How did we forget the one thing we came for?!" Ronald tried to re-open the window only to find it locked from the inside.

"Argh! I made a rookie mistake," he mumbled to himself. "Now I'm acting like the amateur."

Ronald sat on the ground, frustrated and dejected.

"We can't be perfect at everything Ronald."

"I know but this is my career. This is what I live to do. The great Ronald Moore made a terrible mistake."

Susan noticed the disappointment in Ronald's eyes as he stared off into the distance. This was the first time she noticed a crack in his tough guy demeanor. To her own surprise, it pained her to see him that way. The Ronald she knew wouldn't waste time pitying himself. They had a job to do and analyzing past mistakes wouldn't help.

"How about we find another way to get back in," Susan said as she laid a hand on Ronald's shoulder and gave him an encouraging smile. She lifted herself up off the ground and turned to face him. Ronald returned her gaze with a nod, knowing it was time to get back to business.

As he rose from his seat, Susan got an idea. Without Ronald's consent, she took out her gun and fired at the sealed window. The gunshot echoed throughout the land and within the castle's walls.

"Why would you do that?" Ronald asked incredulously. "Now they know where we are."

"Just figured I'd do something you would do." Susan shrugged before climbing through the window.

"I would do? I'm not an idiot," Ronald murmured as he followed her back into the castle.

Just as his feet landed inside the large, circular room, the guards rushed in. Ronald shot two of them, then ducked for cover as a spear nearly grazed him. Susan rushed over to *The Relic of Power* while Ronald distracted the guards. Just as Susan started to put *The Relic of Power* in her backpack, a knife pierced her hand.

"Ugh!" Susan screamed as the relic fell to the floor. Before she could brace herself, the guard shoved her down, picked up *The Relic of Power,* and ran. Susan reached for her gun, aimed, and shot the guard in the back. She slowly stood up and walked over to retrieve *The Relic of Power,* admiring its beauty once again. Just as she opened her backpack, a guard attacked her from behind. Susan's eyes widened as the sting of cold steel pierced her skin. Suddenly, a heavy weight struck her across the head and her eyes closed as she fell to the ground. Ronald, in a fit of rage, slammed the guard to the ground and knocked him upside the head with the end of his pistol. He picked up Susan and *The Relic of Power,* and jumped out the window.

CHAPTER 8

A TRIP TO THE DOCTOR'S OFFICE

Ronald frantically searched for the village as the King's guards chased closely behind. Suddenly, a spear buzzed past his head, throwing him off balance. He tripped and fell to the ground, dropping Susan along the way. Although pain radiated through his entire body, he got back up, put Susan on his back, and fired several rounds of bullets towards the guards that followed.

One guard was so close that Ronald grabbed his spear as he fell to the ground. He ran for several yards, dodging spears while firing behind him. When he felt it was safe, he sat Susan down and threw the spear at one of the guards. He shot two that were closing in on them. A guard tried to attack him from the side but he kicked him in the knee, took his sword, and used it to strike another guard.

Ronald almost thought he was in the clear until he looked past one pile of guards only to see more coming. He grabbed Susan and ran towards the village.

"Excuse me! Move! Move!" Ronald urged as he pushed and shoved people out of his way. He knocked over a small cart and kicked it behind him, entangling one of the guards. Another guard was right beside them and Ronald struggled to run and protect the relic, Susan, and himself.

Unexpectedly, Susan kicked the guard, pulled out her gun and shot him before passing out. Ronald saw a sign for a clinic and rushed inside.

"We need help, now!"

Someone rushed over to him, "Come, come, we can help you."

"Take her first, I can wait," Ronald told the nurse as he looked at his wounds.

"Okay, I'll send Dr. Frownn to help you."

The nurse had Ronald place Susan on one of the beds before directing him to Dr. Frownn's office.

Once inside his office, Dr. Frownn applied pressure to Ronald's wound to stop the bleeding.

"What brings you all this way?" Dr. Frownn asked.

"I'm an explorer," Ronald answered. "I want to explore as much as I can while I can."

"We don't receive many visitors," Dr. Frownn stated. "Nice to have you here. Now, let me just stitch up this wound and you'll be good to go."

In the other room, Susan was also being stitched up. Another doctor cleaned her wound and stopped the bleeding. She awoke just as he sat his needle on a nearby table.

"Where am I?" She asked dazed. "You're at a medical center, getting treated."

"Who are you?" Susan asked weakly.

"I'm Dr. Daws," the doctor replied. Susan fell back asleep from the pain medication Dr. Daws had given her when she arrived. As the doctor went to grab more towels, he tripped and knocked over Susan's bag. Everything fell out, including *The Relic of Power*. He picked it up and walked over to the phone before going into the other room to find Ronald.

"Why is this in your partner's bag?" Dr. Daws held up *The Relic of Power* as he asked the question, but Ronald remained silent.

The energy shifted in the room and Ronald immediately went on high alert. His gut told him that things were about to go left, yet he continued to listen attentively.

"This gives our civilization life," Dr. Daws continued ignoring Ronald's silence. "Without this, we will not be prosperous. It is not for foreigners to come and take. It belongs to the local people. I have called the authorities."

"I should have known!" Ronald exclaimed.

"They're gonna kill us!"

"You are thieves! You will be captured for your crime," Dr. Daws looked at Ronald unsympathetically. Angered by the doctor's actions, Ronald shoved him and grabbed *The Relic of Power* before running into the other exam room to get Susan.

"Wake up! Susan wake up! We have to get out of here!"

"Why?" Susan struggled to open her eyes.

"Because if we don't, we die!" Ronald started to pick her up but she insisted on walking without his help. They grabbed their things and ran towards the door.

Outside the clinic, it was pitch black.

"We need to find somewhere to sleep or at least stay while everything is quiet," said Ronald.

They walked around the city looking for a place until Susan whispered for Ronald to follow her.

"Come over here," she said as she directed him to an abandoned shed. With the flashlight from

Ronald's bag, they saw the tools, bones, and insects in every corner of the neglected space.

"Eww!" shouted Susan as a rat ran across her foot. Ronald shushed Susan and motioned for her to be silent. They stood still hoping no one had heard her outburst.

"Noise will get us killed. Remember that," Ronald warned.

"I understand," agreed Susan. "Now, where are we going to sleep?"

Ronald looked for a clean spot on the floor but couldn't find one.

"We're going to have to make do with what we've got here."

"I brought a blanket," Susan said. "But it's only big enough for one person."

"You use it, I'll be fine." Ronald laid on the dirty floor and stared at the ceiling, trying to still his mind and find peace in the silence. He tried and tried, but thoughts of disappointment were hard to escape. He heard light snoring and turned towards

Susan who had already nodded off to sleep. He grinned to himself, impressed by her growth. He was for certain that before today, she'd be up trying to pick a fight for all the mistakes they made. He sensed she was beginning to trust him more, and it made him feel at ease to know he could trust her too.

Unbeknownst to Ronald and Susan, the remaining leaders at the castle had sent a large, muscular, and very dangerous man to the village to find them. As they were wandering the streets looking for a place to stay, he was also going door to door asking if anyone had seen the two Americans. Almost everyone responded the same, "I don't know," except one woman. She looked up at the man and with a trembling voice answered, "I saw two people go into that shed."

The man looked down at her and asked, "What shed?"

She held up her index finger and pointed to the once-abandoned shed across the street.

Moments later, Ronald saw a shadow growing larger and larger against the shed's wall.

"Who are you?" Ronald jumped up and yelled as the man entered.

"Your doom!" The large man answered with a smirk as he punched a surprised Ronald in the face. Ronald punched him back, followed by a kick in the stomach. Even though he was striking him with all of his might, none of Ronald's hits affected the man.

He picked Ronald up and threw him to a wall. Ronald fell to the ground on impact. The man got down on one knee and punched Ronald repeatedly causing bruises to form all over his aching body. Susan woke up and without the man noticing, pulled out her gun. But before she could fire a shot, he turned and slammed into her. Susan tried to shoot him again but he grabbed the weapon and threw it to the other side of the shed. Susan kept trying to fight him, but he grabbed her right hand

and squeezed it harder and harder as though he planned to break every bone. Ronald grabbed the gun from the other side of the shed and shot the man in his side. He held his side as he doubled over from the pain.

"We have to go, now!" Ronald said to Susan as he gathered his things.

"I agree." Susan got up and threw the blanket into a corner. Ronald took out his phone and called Melody.

"Where's the plane? We need to get out of here."

"When?" Melody asked on the other end of the phone line.

"Now!" Ronald shouted into the phone.

"I'll try to get one out to you within the next three hours," Melody said before hanging up.

Ronald and Susan walked outside to find that it was morning. Before Susan could run across the street, Ronald stopped her.

"Let's go through the back so we don't get caught."

CHAPTER 9

AN ARMY BEHIND ME

Ronald and Susan had to venture through the jungle to get back to the mountain.

Why did I choose this job? Susan thought to herself. Despite her progress, her hope had diminished greatly.

Throughout the mission, Susan tried to remain confident. While she loved idea of an exciting adventure, she had spent most of her life only dreaming of becoming an explorer. She was fulfilling a dream her father had passed down to her. As a young girl, he told her the need for adventure and conquest was in her blood. Her family would never let her forget how great of an explorer her grandfather was and how her father would have followed in his footsteps if not for him being paralyzed after a car accident. She felt she had a destiny to fulfill even though athleticism didn't come as easy as reading and writing for her.

Instead of giving up, she combined her love for learning and exploring and used them in the classroom. She taught lessons on explorers and the historic journeys that resulted in uncovering some of the world's most precious artifacts. Many of her students wanted to become explorers because she introduced them to a new possibility. One they had never considered before sitting in her class.

One day after class, she received a call from Martin that changed her life. A student had written a letter to Ronald about Susan's lessons and how much the class wanted to meet him. The student believed Susan would be a great explorer and asked if Ronald would come to their classroom to meet her and bring some of the artifacts from his expeditions. The letter never made it to Ronald because Martin intercepted it. He did some digging and learned more about Susan's background. Martin admired Susan's grandfather and wondered if she had that level of greatness in her. He gave her a call and discussed a special assignment. He needed someone with her background and knowledge.

Susan knew no amount of research could prepare her for an actual mission. The thought kept her from doing more than teaching. However, when Martin presented her with an opportunity to actually get outside of the classroom and experience it firsthand, she couldn't let it slip away.

Susan reminded herself of how many days and nights she'd spent dreaming about climbing mountains and discovering archaic finds with explorers like Ronald. She was living her wildest dream so she had to give it her all. In that moment, Susan decided doubt would not stop her from completing the mission.

After wandering for an hour, Ronald and Susan made it back to the mountains.

"Shhh," Ronald whispered as trees rustled

nearby. They both crouched down slightly, slowly scanning the area, straining to hear anything that was cause for concern. Suddenly, the sound of limbs breaking beneath thick-soled leather boots surrounded them. The King's soldiers moved in from the left and right as Ronald and Susan sprinted towards the mountain. They climbed, dodging arrows and spears along the way. Just as Ronald shifted to the left to avoid being hit by two arrows, another came from the right and landed in his calf.

"Ugh!" he moaned as he lost his footing and fell, landing painfully on a large boulder. He blinked a few times and shook his head while clutching the arrow and forcefully removing it. Susan saw he was shaken up and headed back down towards him.

"Keep going!" Ronald yelled. "I'll catch up!"

Ronald tried to regain his footing but pieces of the boulder detached, causing him to stumble. He pulled out his climbing axe and stabbed it into the mountain, just as the boulder fell beneath him and on top of four soldiers.

Ronald again started to climb, but the soldiers were at his heels. Three soldiers caught up with him. Ronald pushed one, causing him to lose his grip and fall from the mountain. He tried to fend off the other two soldiers, but failed. One kicked him in his side while another tried to snatch his backpack and force him off the mountain. Ronald focused on not falling but was losing his hold. One of the soldiers held out his leg, ready to charge one final time and force Ronald from the mountain. Instead, the soldier yelled as a woman's size eight combat boot landed on his fingers. Susan stomped once again causing the pained soldier to release his grasp and fall backwards.

Ronald looked to his left to see the other soldier in position to grab at him. Ronald kicked out his left leg, catching the soldier off guard. He kicked again but this time, at a crack in the boulder and it shook and broke apart. The soldier stumbled but was unable to hold on once the bolder fell from the mountain.

"Come on before more come!" Susan yelled as she climbed.

Before Ronald could catch up to her, more soldiers appeared with climbing gear. Ronald and Susan sped up, climbing faster and faster, trying to get to the top before the soldiers reached them. Suddenly, Susan's foot slipped. With quick thinking, she thrust herself into one of the soldiers, grabbing his gear to reposition herself on the side of the mountain. Before she could maneuver out of harm's way, a soldier cut her rope and she fell backwards, landing on a cliff. The soldier rappelled towards her. As he approached, she struggled to retrieve her gun from her bag. Just as he neared, she pointed the gun towards him and he froze. She warned him not to step closer and for a few seconds, he did not move. Then, he took one small step followed by another until he was too close for Susan's comfort.

"Don't move or I'll shoot!" she warned again.

He smirked, feeling more powerful with each second that passed. Susan took a step back, aimed, and fired. The bullet ricocheted off of the mountainside and struck the man in the side. Even with him out of the way, more soldiers headed towards her believing she was vulnerable. As Susan screamed for help, the blade of a soldier's knife caught her before she could dodge it and cut her across the left cheek. She put her hand to her cheek and felt the sting of the small incision. She grew angrier by the second as she stared at the blood sliding from her fingers. Just as the soldier prepared to deliver a fatal blow, Ronald appeared behind him and knocked him off the cliff. Susan slowly got to her feet as Ronald dodged a sword from one soldier on the right and then kicked another soldier in the chest on his left.

"Look out!" Susan yelled as a fiery arrow flew towards Ronald.

Ronald fell to his knees to avoid the flames,

then fired his gun in the direction of the soldier. The soldier ducked and then sent more arrows after them hoping to stop them from moving up the mountain.

The cliff became unstable due to barrage of arrows and started to crumble, with Ronald and Susan still on it. Ronald stabbed his climbing axe into the side of the mountain. As Susan stumbled backwards, he just barely grabbed her hand. Clinging on by only a few fingers, Susan started to slip from his grasp and could see the soldiers waiting below her. "Ronald, get me closer," Susan said motioning to a climbing rope left against the mountain from one of the fallen soldiers. "I'll try," Ronald hoped her plan would work.

With one swift motion, he propelled her towards the hanging robe. She grabbed it and clung to it for a few seconds before willing her body to continue the climb.

Worn and spent, Ronald and Susan climbed, focused on making it to the top and never looking down.

CHAPTER 10

HOME SWEET HOME

Susan stood at the top of the mountain waiting for Ronald.

"You know, the last time we were up here, you were the one telling me to hurry up," Susan boasted.

"You had a rope," Ronald retorted trying to catch his breath as he scaled the final few yards. As he reached the very top, he looked just beyond the mountain range at Melody's approaching helicopter.

"It's time," Susan said to Ronald. She walked closer to the mountain's edge and looked over at the few remaining soldiers.

"Yes, it is," Ronald exhaled deeply as he thought about the past few hours.

The past couple of days had been more than

they both ever imagined and even though they would never admit it, Susan and Ronald had moments when they wondered if they would make it out of Zandina alive.

"Well, look who survived," yelled Melody as she threw down a rope ladder. Ronald grabbed the swaying ladder and held it as Susan climbed up first. Halfway up, he looked out over the rich, vast land of Zandina and considered the truth of their mission. They had taken down an unscrupulous dictator and retrieved one of the world's most powerful artifacts. Usually, he was alone in knowing the truth behind each relic like the near-death experiences, harrowing escapes, and sense of pride at the end. But this time, someone else had been by his side. He could talk through the details and Susan would understand. They'd fought for their lives and won. It was the ultimate success. While Ronald was used to feeling skilled and accomplished after a successful mission, the achievement meant more to him this time but he could not understand why.

On the other hand, Susan couldn't decide if she was more overjoyed about all of the lives she would save by them retrieving *The Relic of Power* or the fact that she had the opportunity to do it in the first place.

As the village faded into a sea of white clouds, the two continued to enjoy a much-earned moment of peace.

About thirty-minutes into the flight, Ronald glanced over at Susan and noticed she was still awake.

"You're not asleep yet? That's a shocker."

Susan rolled her eyes at Ronald's sarcastic comment as it rolled off of her instead of enraging her as it would have in the past.

"Seriously, you were great out there."

Susan finally met his gaze and noticed his soft grin.

"Thanks, Ronald. That means a lot coming

from you," she said appreciatively.

"Believe it or not, I know I'm piece of work. This mission made it clear that I've got some growing up to do. Maybe there are a few things I could learn from a rookie like you."

Susan chuckled to herself before responding. "Okay old man."

"Yeah well, what can I say. We make a pretty good team."

THE NEXT DAY

Martin stood behind the museum, waiting for the plane's door to open. He smiled as Susan and Ronald walked down the stairs and over to where he stood. They walked with less urgency and still appeared slightly disheveled. He peered at the small cut on Susan's cheek.

"You may have to pay extra on this one because we almost died a few times!" Ronald joked.

"Isn't that part of the job?" Martin asked rhetorically. "Susan, are you okay? We can have someone take a look at that cut."

"Oh, it's fine. Just a graze, nothing serious."

"Well, if you change your mind, just let me know," said Martin sincerely.

"Thanks Martin but I'm sure you're more interested in seeing what we found," said Susan.

"Yes, yes! Where is it? I've waited a lifetime for this moment," said Martin enthusiastically.

"I hope it's worth it Martin," Ronald glanced at Martin with a raised brow.

"How was Ronald on the mission?" asked Martin half-jokingly as Susan handed over the mission's prize.

Susan glanced at Ronald and smiled.

"He was the best partner I could possibly have on this mission or any mission."

"That's great to hear," Martin responded surprised. "Now I can assign you with more partners, Ronald."

"Possibly," Ronald said slowly. "But only under one condition."

"I'm listening," replied Martin as he prepared for what Ronald would say next.

"Susan has to come with me," Ronald smiled at Susan as they high-fived.

"Deal!" Martin exclaimed as the three walked towards the museum's rear entrance.

Once inside the private room, Martin carefully placed *The Relic of Power* in a small vault. They stood back and admired the brilliant shades of amber emanating off of the vault's walls from the relic. Even as its inner light transitioned into a subtle flicker, *The Relic of Power* was a sight to behold. Martin keyed in a five-digit code and the vault's door closed. Once it finally shut, all three exhaled a sigh of relief as *The Relic of Power* was out of sight and forever, out of danger.

Special Acknowledgments

I would like to acknowledge family members who were essential in helping me complete my debut book: my mother, Melody Fleming, my brother, Adrian Fleming Jr., my step father, Adrian Fleming, and my father, Eddie Solomon.

A special thank you to my grandparents, Amy and Leonard Roberts, Karolyn Fleming, and Mary Moore as well. To my deceased grandparents, Louise Evans and Sammy Moore, thank you for continuing to look after me from above.

I am grateful for other family members who have helped in this process, Wylene and Bobby Dickey, my wonderful aunt Ruby, Rose and Reddis, Cedric Roberts, Analyce and Elyse Roberts, Chris Walker, Brandon Walker, Redisia Walker, Sunday, Roderick and Roderick Jr. Davis.

Your support is sincerely appreciated.

Thank you to my wonderful teachers, Mrs. Martin, Ms. Troutman, Mr. Lucas, and Dr. Hogan.

To additional family members and friends, thanks for being supportive and helping me celebrate this accomplishment.

Finally, I would like to thank Renita Bryant, Deja Allen, and the Mynd Matters Publishing team for guiding me through the process of revising and publishing ***The Relic of Power***.

Thank you all for reading!

For more information about Keenon Solomon and *The Relic of Power*, visit www.RelicOfPower.com.

www.ingramcontent.com/pod-product-compliance
Lightning Source LLC
Chambersburg PA
CBHW051712180726
48283CB00004B/1316